The Shabbat Princess

Amy Meltzer

Illustrated by

Martha Avilés

KAR-BEN
PUBLISHING

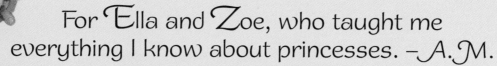

For Ella and Zoe, who taught me
everything I know about princesses. —A.M.

KAR-BEN PUBLISHING
A division of Lerner Publishing Group, Inc.
241 First Avenue North
Minneapolis, MN 55401 USA
1-800-4-Karben

Website address: www.karben.com

Library of Congress Cataloging-in-Publication Data

Meltzer, Amy.
   Shabbat Princess / by Amy Meltzer ; illustrated by Martha Avilés.
      p.   cm.
   Summary: When Rosie pretends to be the Shabbat Princess, invited to her home
along with the Shabbat Queen, she reminds her parents of how they should be
treating their honored guest each week.
   ISBN: 978-0-7613-5142-9 (lib. bdg. : alk. paper)
   ISBN: 978-0-7613-7971-3 (EB pdf)
[1. Sabbath—Fiction. 2. Judaism—Customs and practices—Fiction. 3. Family life—
Fiction.] I. Avilés Junco, Martha, ill. II. Title.
PZ7.M51646Sh 2011
[E]—dc22   2010020302

Manufactured in the United States of America
3 – CG – 2/1/15

"The Shabbat is a Queen, whose arrival changes the humblest home into a palace."

—Talmud, Shabbat, 199a

It was Friday afternoon, and Rosie's mother was setting the table for Shabbat. Rosie followed closely behind, folding cloth napkins into perfect triangles.

"Why do we always use our best dishes for Shabbat?" Rosie asked.

"Because we're welcoming the Shabbat Queen!" answered her mother. "And a queen deserves only the best."

Rosie liked queens. She really did. But she loved princesses. "This week, could we invite the Shabbat Princess, too?" she asked. "Princesses are much more exciting than queens."

"I've never heard of a Shabbat Princess," said her mother. She turned to Rosie's father. "Have you?"

He shook his head. "Nope. No such thing."

Rosie frowned. "How can there be a Shabbat Queen, but no Shabbat Princess?"

Her mother thought for a moment. "Can you be our Shabbat Princess?"

"Me? The Shabbat Princess?" asked Rosie. She looked down at her blue jeans and t-shirt. Not very princess-y. "I'll be right back!" she called, as she dashed up the stairs to her bedroom.

Rosie opened her dress-up box and spread her fanciest costumes across the bed. She studied each piece thoughtfully. This outfit had to be just right.

She chose a purple satin gown and a pair of silver slippers.

She added her finest pieces of jewelry and placed a tiara on her head.

Rosie studied herself in the mirror and decided she looked perfect.

When her father saw her come down the stairs, he sounded an imaginary trumpet. "Announcing......the Shabbat Princess!"

Rosie's face lit up. Being a Shabbat Princess felt like a very important job. But where was her castle?

"We need a moat," she declared.

"I don't think so," replied her father.

"A tower?"

Her mother shook her head.

No one in Rosie's family seemed to understand princesses. "If only I had a fairy godmother," she sighed.

Rosie's mother took her hand and gave it a gentle squeeze. "I may not be a fairy godmother, but I'm sure we can make things a *little* more regal. Let's go have a look at the table."

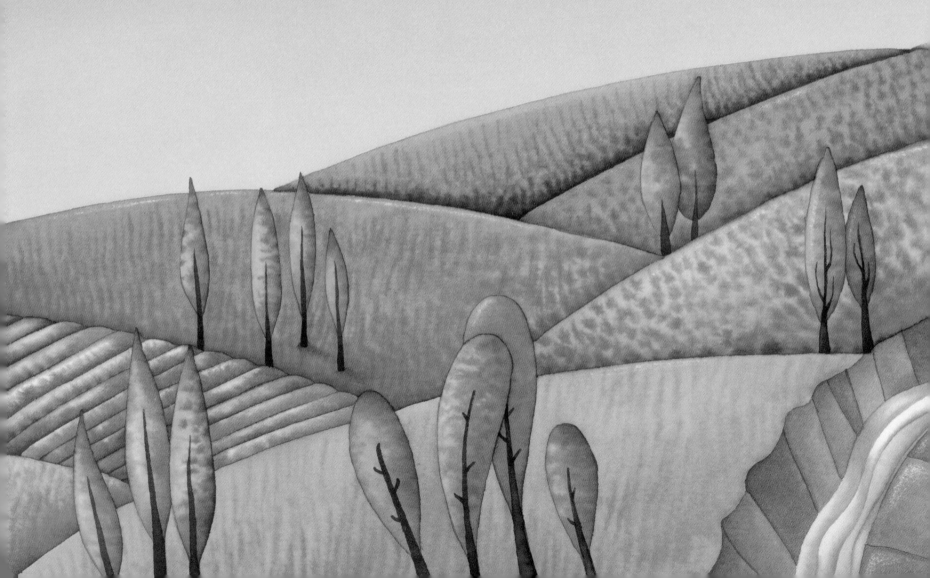

Rosie and her mother walked into the dining room. Rosie looked at the sturdy brass candlesticks. "Do we have anything with diamonds?" she asked hopefully.

"No diamonds," said her mother. "But your Aunt Carole gave us a set of crystal candlesticks for our wedding. I tucked them away because I was afraid they would get broken. Let's go look for them."

"Perfect!" replied Rosie.

Rosie's mother took an enormous box
down from the hall closet. She and Rosie
unwrapped layers and layers of tissue
paper. Carefully, they pulled out the tall
glass candlesticks and placed them on
the table.

This was a definite improvement. But next to the sparkly candlesticks, the Kiddush cup looked dull. "Do we have any silver goblets?" asked Rosie.

Her father raised one eyebrow. "This goblet *is* silver."

"Are you sure?" asked Rosie. "I thought silver was supposed to be shiny."

Rosie's father sighed and rolled up his sleeves. "I suppose it could use some polish."

A few minutes later he returned from the kitchen. He took a deep bow as he placed the Kiddush cup on the table. "The royal goblet, Your Highness."

Next to the gleaming Kiddush cup the pink napkin covering the challah looked plain. Rosie shook her head. "Princesses do not like *plain*," she declared. "Do we have anything made of velvet? Or satin?"

"I don't think so," said her mom, rummaging through the bureau.

"I have an idea." Rosie exclaimed. She zipped back up the stairs.

Rosie returned with an armful of glittery, sequined, scarves.

"Which one do you like best?" she asked her parents.

After laying a golden scarf atop the two loaves of challah, the family stood back and admired their work.

"This is a Shabbat table fit for a princess," proclaimed Rosie's father. "And not a moment too soon. It's almost sundown."

Rosie's family gathered around the table and lit the candles. The flames danced on the curves of the crystal.

Her father raised the Kiddush cup and sang the blessing. Rosie saw the beautiful grapevines on the sides of the shiny goblet.

Her mother lifted the shimmering challah cover with a flourish, and together they recited the blessing.

After dinner, everyone agreed that the meal had felt like a truly royal banquet.

Rosie looked up at her parents. "Do you think the Shabbat Queen is angry?" Rosie wondered.

"Why would she be angry?" asked her father.

"Well, we made everything so much fancier for the Shabbat Princess than we usually do for the Queen."

Rosie's mother and father exchanged glances. "No," said her mother. "I'm certain that she's not angry. In fact, I think she is delighted."

"Why?" Rosie asked.

"Because the Shabbat Princess reminds us of something important. When an honored guest visits our house, she deserves extra-special treatment."

"So can we build that moat?" asked Rosie.

"No moat," smiled her mother. "But the sparkly candlesticks can stay."

"And I'll polish the Kiddush cup every week," added her father.

"And I'll still wear my tiara and gown every now and then," said Rosie. "So the Shabbat Queen can feel right at home."

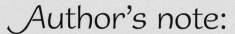

Author's note:

When the Israelites were wandering in the wilderness, with only the few possessions they had brought from Egypt, they gave their most treasured items to build a beautiful tabernacle, a house of worship to God. From this, we learn the concept of "hiddur mitzvah" — the enhancement of mitzvot and observances with objects of beauty.

Amy Meltzer is an award-winning Jewish educator and a pioneer in the field of Jewish environmental education. She is also the author of *A Mezuzah on the Door* (Kar-Ben). A native of Baltimore, she lives in Northampton, Massachusetts with her husband, daughters, and dog, Zev.

Martha Avilés was born and raised in Mexico City. She has illustrated many children's books including *Say Hello, Lily* (Kar-Ben).

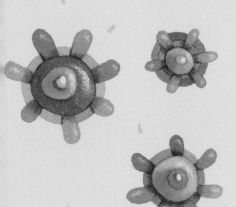
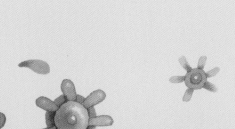